How to make a robot:

fig. 1

fig. 2

fig. 3

How to dismantle a robot:

fig. 1

fig. 2

fig. 3

The Trouble with SISTERS and robots

Steve Gritton

Albert Whitman & Company, Morton Grove, Illinois

Library of Congress Cataloging-in-Publication Data

Gritton, Steve.
The trouble with sisters and robots / by Steve Gritton.
p. cm.
Summary: After frantically trying to stop his out of control robot from turning
everything it touches into metal, Kyle finally listens to his little sister's advice.
ISBN 978-0-8075-8090-5
[1. Robots—Fiction. 2. Brothers and sisters—Fiction.] I. Title.
PZ7.G89113Tr 2009   [E]—dc22   2008055705

Text and illustrations copyright © 2009 by Steve Gritton.
Published in 2009 by Albert Whitman & Company,
6340 Oakton Street, Morton Grove, Illinois 60053-2723.
Printed in China.
10 9 8 7 6 5 4 3 2 1

For more information about
Albert Whitman & Company, please visit our
web site at www.albertwhitman.com.

For Lyssa,
who gave me the nudge, well, it was more like a push . . .
OK, it was a shove. —SG

Kyle's sister, Lizzy, was always in the way. When he went to the park or the pool—or even when he did his homework—she was there. So it was no surprise that when Kyle headed into the backyard to look for buried treasure, Lizzy tagged along.

Kyle surveyed the yard.

"Let's dig here," suggested Lizzy.

"Be quiet, Lizzy!" said Kyle.

Kyle found a good spot to start digging. Soon he had dug a good-sized hole.

"You know, when Mom sees this—" Lizzy began.

"Be quiet, Lizzy!"

Then, KLANG! Kyle's shovel hit something hard.

There, staring up at him, was the head of a robot! Kyle picked it up and cleaned it off. The head was in good shape except for one rusty eye.

Kyle had a brilliant idea. "I will make a robot," he proclaimed. He carried the head to the garage and gathered all the scrap metal he could find. He spent the rest of the morning in his bedroom, attaching the pieces to the robot head.

He had just finished when Lizzy walked in.

"Oooh, nice robot. I think you should call it—"

"Quiet, Lizzy!" snapped Kyle. "His name is Rusteye."

Kyle took an extra-long extension cord and plugged Rusteye in. The robot sputtered to life. *It works!* thought Kyle.

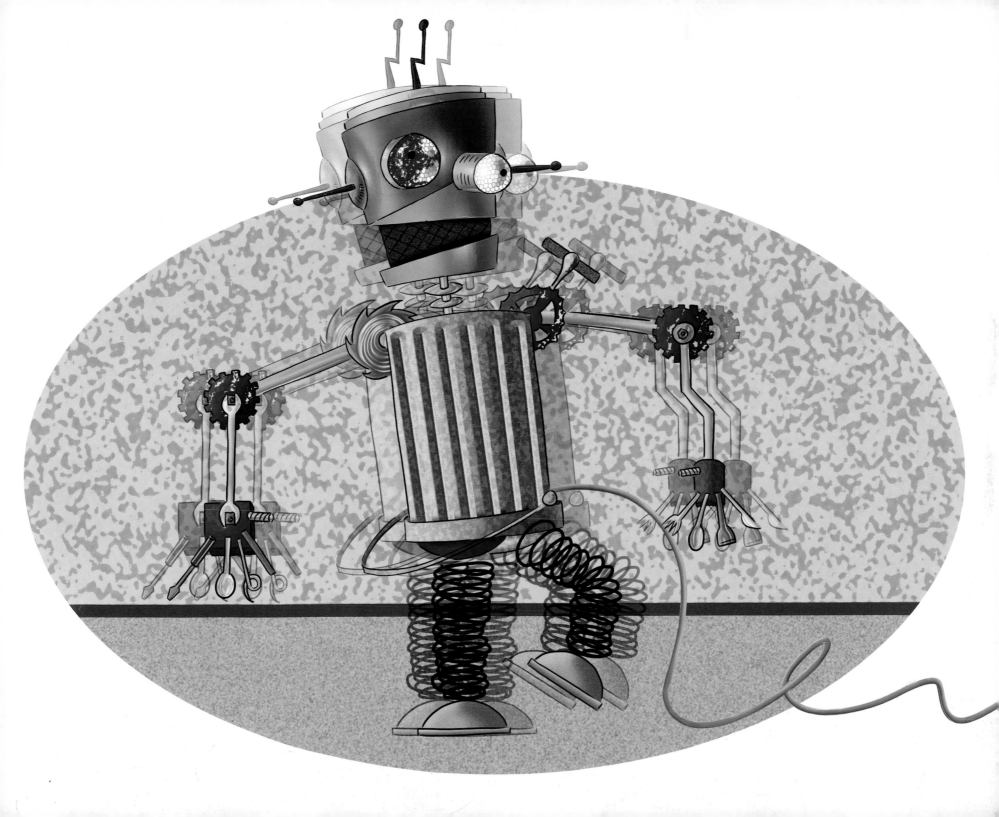

At first, Rusteye just stood there, looking around the room.

Kyle tossed his basketball to the robot. Rusteye caught it easily. Then his head began to glow.

Kyle and Lizzy took a step backwards. Suddenly, the orange basketball turned silver.

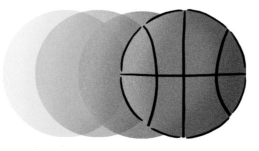

Rusteye dropped the ball with a loud thud.

The ball rolled in front of Lizzy. "It's metal!" she declared. "That robot head must be magic!"

"Be quiet, Lizzy!"

Rusteye reached over and touched Kyle's desk. His head began to glow again. The pencils, paper, even the erasers turned to polished steel.

"Uh-oh!" said Lizzy.

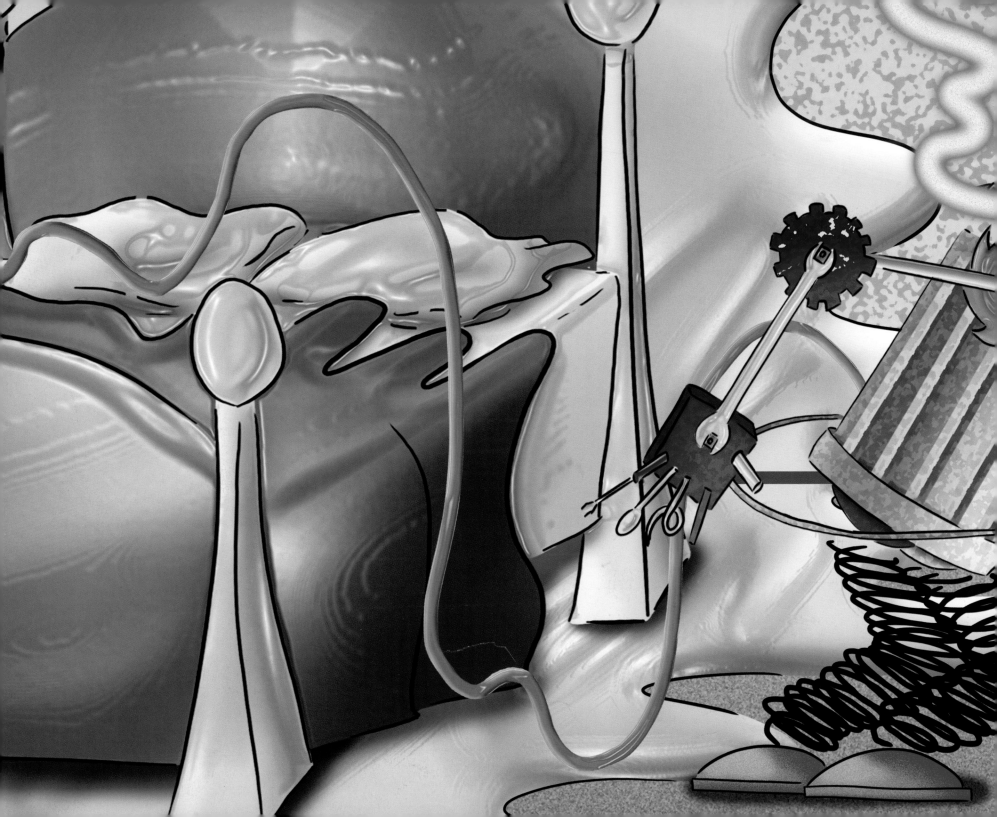

Before they knew it, Rusteye had touched everything in the room. The bed, the rug, the door, and the walls were now shiny metal.

Then Sasha, the cat, walked in. Rusteye reached down . . .

"NO!" shouted Kyle and Lizzy. But Sasha was now a metallic statue.

"I have to stop Rusteye! How can I do that without getting touched?" Kyle said in panic.

Lizzy said, "Well, you could just—"

"Be quiet, Lizzy!"

Kyle and Lizzy chased Rusteye
down the hall and down the stairs.
Everything in his wake turned to metal.

They caught up with him in the kitchen, where their mom and dad were enjoying their morning coffee. "Mom, Dad! Look out!" Kyle yelled. But he was too late. Mom and Dad sat frozen at the table.

"Oh, no!" cried Lizzy.

"I don't know what to do!" said Kyle.

"Well, you could just—" said Lizzy again.

"Gosh, Lizzy—BE QUIET!"

By now, Rusteye had ventured out into the backyard. The grass, the trees, and the fence were gleaming silver.

"Where's Max?" asked Lizzy. They both looked for the family dog. Then Kyle found him. Max had been standing next to a tree, doing, um . . . his business, when Rusteye came by.

"This is getting worse! How do I stop him?" said Kyle.

Lizzy tried again. "You could just—"

"I'm thinking, Lizzy! Be quiet!" Kyle said.

They followed Rusteye into the front yard. What a sight! Every tree, bush, house—and even the street—had been turned into metal. The mailman and his mail had met the same fate.

"AAAARGH!" shouted Kyle. "He's turning the whole neighborhood into metal! Lizzy, what can I do?"

"Are you going to tell me to be quiet?" asked Lizzy.

"No."

"Are you sure?"

"Yes!"

"OK! You could just unplug him!"

Could it be that simple? Kyle thought. They followed the extension cord through the backyard, into the kitchen (Hi, Mom, Hi, Dad), up the stairs, down the hall, and into Kyle's room.

Kyle stared at the plug for a second, closed his eyes, and pulled.

There was a flash of electricity. Just for a second, nothing happened. Then, slowly the room began to change back to normal.

Even Sasha, though a little dazed, became her old self.

Kyle and Lizzy followed
the changes through the house
and down the street. There they found
Rusteye standing motionless. He had been
trying to touch Mrs. McGillicutty, who was
hitting him with her cane.

Kyle and Lizzy looked at each other and smiled. They had stopped Rusteye! Then Kyle gave Lizzy the biggest hug a brother could give.

"You know what, Lizzy? I'm glad you were with me," Kyle confessed.

They carried Rusteye home, took off his head, and buried it in the backyard.

Kyle never told his sister to be quiet again . . .

Except when she made him play tea party and wear a silly hat.
And then she couldn't stop laughing.
"BE QUIET, LIZZY!"

How to make a robot:

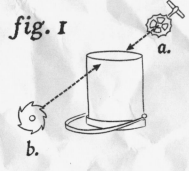

fig. 1

a.

b.

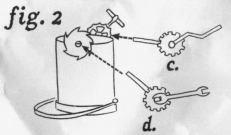

fig. 2

c.

d.

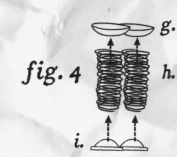

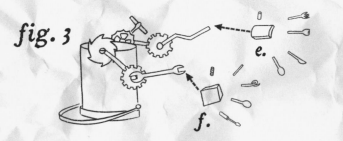

fig. 3

e.

f.

fig. 4

g.

h.

i.

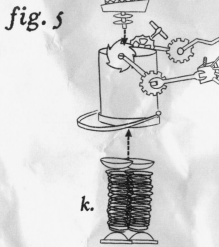

fig. 5

j.

k.

How to dismantle a robot:

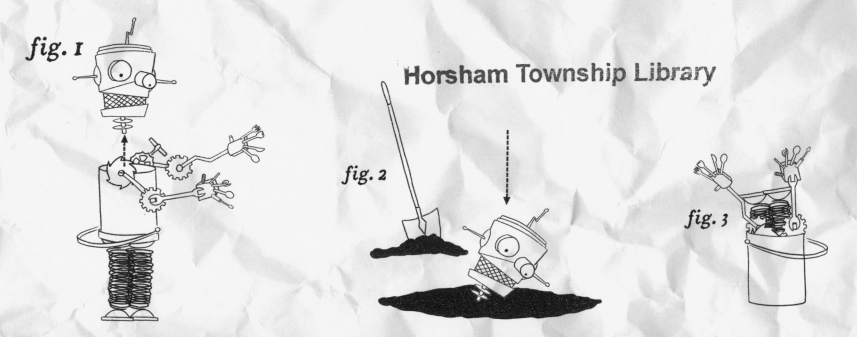

fig. 1

fig. 2

fig. 3